GILBERT'S
GOBSTOPPER

To Sally and Ella

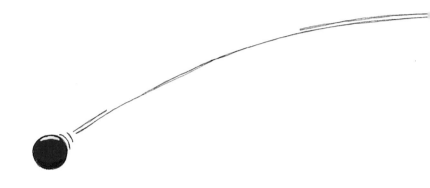

First published in the United States 1988
by Dial Books for Young Readers
A Division of NAL Penguin Inc.
2 Park Avenue · New York, New York 10016
Originally published in Great Britain
by Hamish Hamilton Children's Books
Copyright © 1988 by Mark Haddon
Printed in Great Britain
First edition
OBE
2 4 6 8 10 9 7 5 3 1

Library of Congress Cataloging in Publication Data
Haddon, Mark. Gilbert's Gobstopper.
Summary: Follows the adventures of Gilbert's
amazing Gobstopper as it travels from his mouth to
the bottom of the sea to the wilds of outer space.
[1. Candy—Fiction.] I. Title.
PZ7. H1165Gi 1988 [E] 87-19961
ISBN 0-8037-0506-9

GILBERT'S GOBSTOPPER

Mark Haddon

Dial Books for Young Readers · New York

TIME PASSES....